FIGHT
For Me

Fight For Me

L. Clara

Content warnings include but are not limited to:

Sexually explicit scenes - as in two men - do you really need more of a warning?

BDSM

Internalized homophobia

Doctor/patient relationship

Violence (MMA fights)

Mention of past Child Physical Abuse

Depression

If any of these could be triggering, please skip this title. Your mental health is more important than this book.

For anyone who has been doom scrolling on social media
and thought... "Bow chicka wow wow"

You're welcome.

Please keep in mind that this book is a work of romantic fiction. This is not a guide to BDSM, nor is it a suggestion to date your doctor. The idea for this book came after I was mindlessly scrolling social media. Enjoy!

Playlist

Goosebumps - Remix ~ L E Travis Scott, HVME

Do It To It ~ J ACRAZE, Cherish

Where Are You Now ~ Lost Frequencies, Calum Scott

Peru ~ Fireboy DML, Ed Sheeran

Love Tonight (David Guetta Remix) Shouse, David Guetta

Crazy What Love Can Do ~ David Guetta, Becky Hill, Ella Henderson

Wasted Love (feat. Lagique) ~ Ofenbach, Lagique

When I'm Gone (with Katy Perry) ~ Alesso, Katy Perry

Tell It To My Heart ~MEDUZA, Hozier

Rise ~ Lost Frequencies

Bad Habits ~ (Ed Sheeran)

My Head & My Heart ~ Ava Max

Breaking Me ~ Topic, A7S

Take You Dancing ~ Jason Derulo

KiSS My (Uh Oh) ~ Anne-Marie, Little Mix

Love Again ~ Dua Lipa

Let's Love ~ David Guetta, Sia

For My Hand (feat. Ed Sheeran) ~ Burna Boy, Ed Sheeran

HOYT

This has always been my least favorite part.

The plane's engine roars beneath my feet as we begin our descent to the ground. If I'm honest, flying in general has never been in my top five ways to travel. I mean, have you seen *Final Destination*? Unfortunately, when I have a match scheduled in a country on the other side of the world, there is no other option.

I grip the ends of the armrest as I close my eyes and press my head against the back of my seat. A strong but smooth impact startles me to alertness when we finally hit the landing strip. I let out a ragged breath when the captain's commanding voice sounds over the intercom.

"Welcome to Las Vegas. Local time is nine-twenty-three am. We thank you for flying with us today, Mr. Beck. We hope to see you on Private Skies International again soon." A soft crackle takes over the airway before he disconnects the microphone.

I sense George at my side before I look in that direction. His knowing smile grates my nerves.

"Why do I keep you around when, after all this time, you still fuck with me after a flight?" I grumble as I stand to my full height, or almost my full height. I'm a bit too tall to stand fully on the plane. "My fear of flying is your granddaughter's fault, old man."

"If I remember correctly, kid, it was just as much your idea to watch that stupid ass movie as it was hers." George's deep, boisterous laugh brings a smile to my face, and he claps a hand on my shoulder as we move to the plane's exit.

I roll my eyes and let my mind drift back to the night he's talking about.

"Just because you were older than her, you thought you could handle it when you were as skittish as a stray cat in heat back then."

For all the shit the old man gives me, he'll never know how truly grateful I am for taking me in all those years ago. He didn't have to help out a bloodied up kid from Brooklyn, wandering the streets after getting the crap kicked out of him, yet again, by his foster dad. But George did. And he's been by my side ever since.

A smartass response is on the tip of my tongue but dies quickly when I reach the door. Bright sunshine blinds me, and I'm hit with the obnoxious desert heat. I squint my eyes into slits as I fight to see until I drag my sunglasses down from where they sit on top of my head.

"Welcome to Vegas," I murmur to myself while I make my way down the steps. I freeze when I see her standing on the tarmac. Her bright blue hair is piled high in a messy bun, and she's wearing her go-to combo of a tank top and yoga pants. Unless we have an event to attend, she keeps it casual. A wide smile splits her lips when she catches a glimpse my face. I stride down the steps and cross the distance toward her. My arms fold around her, lifting her into the air.

"Oh my god you brute, put me down. It's been less than a week." Lexi squeals and slaps my shoulders. "I saw the match; you did good like always. But what the hell happened with the pussy that bailed last minute?" she asks. Her lack of filter is something I've come to appreciate over the years.

George appears before I can continue, and her attention instantly goes to her grandfather, enveloping him in a bear hug rivaling ours. Their relationship has always been one I've envied. He may have taken me in and treated me as his own all these years, but I never had the chance to know my own grandparents. They died years before I lost my parents.

"You know, the only reason this boy hugged you so tightly is because you're the first person he's seen after stepping off a plane." I can hear him fighting back laughter as he speaks into her shoulder.

Footsteps pad toward us at an unnatural speed, and it would have me on edge if I didn't know Corbin had fallen asleep on the flight. A loud yawn is his only greeting before Lexi gestures toward the waiting car service she organized for us.

"Hey C." She punches his biceps, always having to remind him she can take him.

While they may have only dated in high school, their competitive nature continues to bring them back to one another. Even if it's only for a night at a time. A low grumble sounds from his chest as he pulls her under his arm.

"I missed you too, Lex." I hear the smack of a kiss followed closely by a grunt when she presumably sucker punches him in the gut.

George takes it upon himself to step between the two. He may know that we're all sexually active considering my reputation and the others are in their late twenties, but he actively avoids the topic.

"We'll take this car." George gestures toward a black sedan before he drags Corbin behind him. The two of them will spend the entire car ride talking techniques and training strategies while Lexi and I need to talk about other matters. To make it easier on all of us, Lex always orders two cars for us after trips like this. "See you both at the hotel." He wraps Lexi in a quick hug before releasing her and slides into the back seat of the waiting car.

Not long after everyone's luggage is loaded into the waiting SUV, Lexi and I are off. She sits cross-legged, facing me on the seat with her phone in hand while she details what I missed while at the event she was forced to stay behind for.

"The most exciting portion of the auction was the training session you had up for grabs." Her phone drops into her lap as she claps her hands excitedly. "There was a slap fight between a twink and a redhead. Yes, just like the song, it was epic!"

She goes into even more detail about how vicious the two became; her laughter is infectious, which makes me join in with her. My amusement turns to shock when she tells me they're best friends and agreed to share me instead of fighting over me.

"Uh, they do realize that I'm not fucking either of them, right?"

My throat bobs as I gulp back the worry. I may be the only openly pansexual KOC fighter, but even with my playboy reputation, I've made it a point not to fuck around with any charity auction winners. It feels too dirty.

"Eh, they know your rules, but you know how people can be." She shrugs before continuing to speed through the highlights. "I fucked Elijah, oh, and you have the Trevor Project event before the next fight."

Lexi has her phone back in her hands and is scrolling through social media by the time she stops speaking. My excitement about hanging out with the kids from The Trevor Project is put on the back burner when I realize what she said. I place my large hand over hers and cover the device.

"You fucked Elijah? As in Elijah "The Smolder" Stewart? The CEO of the franchise? The man who owns Knock Out Championship?" My jaw is barely off the ground given the shock and confusion clouding my mind after the admission.

Xander

Two weeks ago

"Are you fucking kidding me, Xander?" Owen, my boss, screams while he reads the letter of resignation I handed him ten minutes ago. "You were supposed to take over for me so I could retire, not leave me to train someone else! What the fuck, kid?"

Owen drags a hand through his silver hair. I had no idea he expected me to take over for him. Especially after I've told him time after time that I needed more excitement. I spent years in school getting my degree. I've never been great at sports, so becoming a doctor in sports medicine was the closest I could hope to get to the field. Unfortunately, I was hired as a sports medical practitioner. Mostly for my assistance in physical therapy for the US Olympic Swim Team, which is great in theory. Working for an Olympic team is the highest level I could get to. But swim teams are notorious for having the least injuries in my field. They also don't need much physical therapy outside of training.

"Listen, this is an opportunity that I won't get again. I can't turn it down," I reply with confidence.

Working for the KOC will give me all the excitement I crave and not the same mundane tasks every day just so I don't lose the knowledge my degree has given me. Plus, there's little to no chance of snow in Vegas, which just sounds like a good time to me.

"Whatever, kid. Don't bother staying through the notice," Owen grumbles, *"I can't bear to look at you. Get out."*

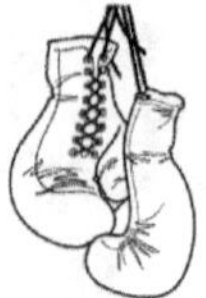

Present Day

"Thank you again!"

I'm unable to hide my excitement as I stroll out of the leasing office. I toss the key to my new apartment in the air and catch it before I return to my car and park in my official spot on the other side of the building. The moving truck will be here in a few hours, so I have time to unload what I have in my car.

My excitement mounts as soon as I push the door open to my new home. One I've yet to see in person since I was living on the other side of the country. It's modern with bright white walls and floor-to-ceiling windows that allow so much natural light into the space. I take a moment to absorb the layout of my new space. The most gorgeous and the lightest color of hardwood floors I've ever seen cover the open room. It reminds me of the sand on a Caribbean beach.

I spend the next few hours unloading my car while I wait for the moving company to arrive with everything else. Thankfully, my employment agreement with KOC included professional movers. I'm pretty sure, since I'm not used to this heat, I'd die of heat stroke before I got all my possessions unloaded on my own. Plus, once the movers arrive, I spend my time directing three unfairly beautiful, ripped men to where my stuff should go. They work quickly, and I'm shocked when, after two hours of them unloading, I'm alone.

Before I bother doing anything else, I grab my toolbox and set my sights on my bed. It's my favorite piece of furniture and the one thing I splurged on when I started my career. The frame looks innocent enough, but the headboard is something I had custom-built. It's a beautiful red leather with heavy-duty metal rings bolted onto either side. What can I say? I enjoy control with my partners . . . at least in the bedroom.

I feel a sense of accomplishment when the bed is finally back together and in place. The red sheet set I found matches the leather headboard, and the deep grey comforter completes the look, bringing everything together.

A loud grumble from my stomach reminds me I forgot to eat today with all the excitement, so I grab my phone from the counter, opening the delivery app. I do a double take when it tells me I have a free appetizer for my birthday. Shit, the days have all blurred together, and with the anticipation of the move, I completely forgot. Not that I do much for my birthday any other year, but this year feels different.

It's my twenty-ninth birthday.

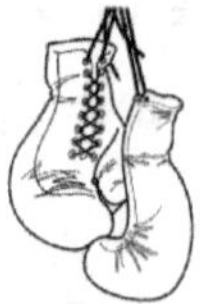

The decision to explore the new city I call home is an easy one. Some might've found it daunting, but not me. With the community I was in and having to hide so much of myself, I'm not be ready to shout my sexuality from the rooftops. However, being in a new place where I don't know anyone makes me more comfortable and willing to live my truth.

The bass bumps wildly as I enter the club. Neon lights flash while people crowd together on the dance floor. Unable to hide my smile as I take in my surroundings, I meander to the bar in no real hurry and lean against it with my elbows resting on the black granite top while I patiently wait for someone to take my drink order.

A man who looks like he should be on the cover of GQ magazine strides toward me with purpose and a sinful grin spread across his stupidly gorgeous face. Fuck, is everyone in this city good-looking?

"What can I get for ya?" he asks with a subtle wink.

I struggle to remember what I wanted to drink and blurt something about a shot.

"You got it, handsome." His flirtatious response stuns me.

I've not been around many open-minded people, let alone men confident enough in their masculinity or sexuality to flirt without a confirmation of the other person's status. His eyes stay locked on mine as he pours the tequila into a glass and hands it over with a suggestive wink before disappearing back into the sea of other guests seeking liquid courage.

I shoot the liquid back without a second thought, my tongue darting out to lick up the excess before I return my gaze to the dance floor. A slim woman with vibrant blue hair and eyes to match approaches me with a warm smile. She's absolutely stunning in a black minidress with cutouts across her chest. The fabric is dotted with sequins, which make her sparkle under the neon lights.

"Hi, I'm Lexi," the blue-haired beauty introduces herself. "Please tell me you're here alone because I'm tired of the sausage and taco fest hanging around my friends. I just want to dance."

She gestures up to the VIP area where I see two sexy as hell men sitting comfortably on a couch while a swarm of women and men are dancing around them, vying for their attention. The raven-haired man looks familiar. He's buff and, from what I can see, at least partially covered in ink.

A chuckle rumbles free from my chest as I hold out my hand to introduce myself. "Xander, it's nice to meet you. I just moved to town so, yes, I'm here alone," I confirm.

Her smile grows when she clasps my hand and pulls me along with her. Never one to shy away from the dance floor, I begin to move. The music flows through me as I move with the beat. Lexi giggles and places her hands on my chest while she leans in close enough to speak into my ear.

"Finally, someone who can keep up with me!" she cheers happily.

I take her hand and lead her through the dance floor as we dominate the space. When she decides to grind her ass against my dick, I feel regret for the first time that I really don't like women sexually. I've dated my share of women after feeling pressure from outside forces. Sure, things had become physical, but only after I watched a few gay porn videos. And fucking them from behind was the only way I could get off.

It makes me an ass, I know, but it's part of the reason I'm so excited to be here. I'm less likely to be judged for my sexuality when I decide to make it known. The only gay sexual experience I've had was with someone I met through a hookup app. It was fun, and he was fantastic, but neither of us were ready for anything serious considering the mindset of the small town we lived in.

A large hand clasps her shoulder and spins her around. I glance up to see one of the men she had gestured to earlier.

"It's time to get out of here, Lex," a deep, gruff voice interrupts. My eyes go wide when I see that it belongs to the blond guy she had pointed out earlier, who is now standing next to her. "We have an early event before the weigh-in."

Lexi nods and gracefully steps away in her ridiculously high heels while she waves her fingers at me. I can't help but smirk as I make my way to the exit when I realize just how late it is. My eyes lift toward the door to find the other man my new friend had pointed out to me earlier. As soon as he realizes I'm watching him, he winks with a subtle nod before dipping out into the night.

HOYT

The kitchen's floor-to-ceiling windows at the KOC training facility allows the early morning sun to shine into the room. I bask in the warmth of the sun while standing under an air vent as I wait for my victims. A chuckle escapes, knowing that the people who bid on a training session never actually want to do the work. They expect me to be up in their personal space, which will never happen. It's a line I will not cross.

I glance up to see Lexi is being followed by what she accurately described as a redhead and a twink. A smile tugs at my mouth as I shake my head. My best friend catches sight of me and can't hide her laughter at my reaction to the newcomers.

"Paige, Donovan."—she pauses and steps aside so that they can see me entirely.—"This is my friend, Hoyt Beck." Lexi gestures to me in greeting.

Paige is a looker. She's completely stacked with perky tits and a round ass, and given any other circumstance, I'd have her bent over a weight bench even with a room full of people as she begs me for more. Her counterpart, Donovan, is just as sexy, slim but fit, and based on the outline in his shorts, he has plenty to work with.

Lexi doesn't get a chance to finish the introduction before the squealing starts.

"Oh my god! It's really you!" Paige, the cute redhead, exclaims at the same moment she leaps onto me. To keep her from landing on her ass, I instinctively wrap my arms around her.

The other half of this dynamic duo rolls his pretty eyes while I try to lower Paige to her feet. She latches onto my biceps, nails digging into my flesh as she tries to hold on to me. Donovan groans with frustration and steps forward to pull the girl off of me.

"Bitch, you have no sense of decorum," he speaks for the first time; his voice is deep but has a femininity to it I find endearing.

Suddenly she's pulled from me, leaving scratches on my arms. I can't help but be amused by the irony of her leaving marks on me when she's one of the few I meet who will never have the opportunity to do so in the way she so obviously wants.

"I'm so sorry about her, Hoyt. She's never been around people before. I just found her on the street and have been trying to teach her how to act like a productive member of society instead of a feral cat, but as you can tell, it hasn't been going well."

Laughter erupts from everyone in the room, apart from Paige. She looks like a bee has stung her. When we finally get control over our amusement at her expense, I take over.

Once I determine how much experience the two of them have with gym equipment, I decide the best option is to start out slow with some cardio. I lead them through a circuit of free weights and machines with a little bit of a cardio boost in between. The alarm on my watch goes off when our hour-long training session finally comes to an end, and I couldn't be happier.

Mental exhaustion is a real thing, more so than physical after the training sessions I offer up in these charity auctions. Paige and Donavon haven't quite taken the hint to leave even though our training has ended. The two of them park themselves on stools to sit on either side of me at the smoothie bar; inviting themselves to stay and hang out. Lexi, the beautiful woman she is, chimes in when she sees what's happening.

"I got you fresh cottage cheese." She winks at me.

I stand to stride around the bar, which is stocked with anything we may need after a workout. My lips turn up into a sly grin as I pull a few items out of the refrigerator.

"Would y'all like a protein shake? I'm making my favorite." I offer as genuinely as I can muster while I place items in a row so they can see the concoction I'm making. Donovan is the first one to gag when I place cottage cheese, kale, skim milk, and protein powder on the counter next to the blender. When I look up again, the space is empty.

Corbin is cackling, unable to control the giddiness over my go-to protein concoction scaring off yet another stage five clinger . . . or set of clingers in this case. Lexi shakes her head with a growing smile as she puts everything except the kale away and pulls out fresh spinach, sugarless powdered peanut butter, and a banana. It may seem odd, but the combination tastes like a Reese's peanut butter cup.

"So, what is the plan for the rest of the day?" I turn to Lexi after I finish my drink.

She looks up from her phone and glares daggers from where she sits across from me. We sit in silence for a moment before she rolls her eyes.

"I agreed to be your social media manager, not your personal assistant," she grumbles while tapping furiously on her screen. "You're lucky I love your stupid ass, ya brute."

Her refusal to accept that she's taken over as my personal assistant only makes the situation more fun for me. She hated someone else having control over my schedule, so she scared Erika off. Lexi huffs out a breath before going into the details of what my day looks like. Weigh-in is in an hour, and she graciously left time for me to sleep, considering how late we were out. Then the event tonight. Overall, it should be an easy and uneventful day.

Xander

Creamy, bittersweet liquid scalds my tongue as I take a sip of the much-needed caffeine in my thermos. The familiar face of my new boss, Gavin, greets me when I step inside the KOC complex. His thick blond hair is hidden under a backwards cap, while his green eyes sparkle in the sunlight – what? I may have done some research on my new boss, he may be in his late fifties but you'd never be able to tell from the staff directory picture. Gavin's grin is infectious the moment he sees me. I chuckle as I close the distance between us and hold my hand out in greeting. He eagerly shakes it before leading me to where I'll be stationed most of the time.

Once we're in my office, he takes a seat in front of my desk while I get myself situated and confirm that my passwords work for the tablet and laptop they provided. He explains a little bit of what to expect today and then abruptly clears his throat.

"Listen, I hate to do this." He smiles apologetically. "But Parker called out sick, so instead of taking you under my wing like I normally would, you'll have to handle the physicals yourself. Do you think you're up for the challenge?"

My mouth turns up at the corners, and I nod excitedly. "It's been way too long since I've had any kind of challenge. Let's do it," I confirm.

Gavin leads me to the exam room I'll be using today. After he apologizes again for sending me into the lion's den without at least a day to shadow him, I wave him off to prepare what I need and check the medical history of who I'll be seeing today.

The morning goes by in a flash with no hiccups. Every fighter is welcoming and kind. I appreciate it, given how much information I have to take down in a limited amount of time. It's not until the second to last patient of the day sits on my table and I see the annoyance in his eyes that I realize the day won't be as smooth sailing as I hoped.

Callum Westbrook sits on my table with his arms crossed tightly against his chest. The position makes it nearly impossible for me to do the exam needed to make sure he's fit to proceed with the evening's fight.

"Hi Callum, I'm Doctor Xander Dawson." I offer a hand, which he doesn't bother to acknowledge. Alrighty then, it's my first day and already with a hardass. "You can call me Xander or Dr. Dawson, either is fine."

"I get it. You've done physicals before every fight. You're sick of it." I pause for dramatic effect. "Your job is to go out there and fight, yeah?" I wait for a response and am ignored yet again, so I continue. "Well, mine is to make sure you're healthy enough to do so. Here's the deal. You either let me check you over or I'm going to have them mark you as medically forfeiting all matches until further notice." I take a step back and mimic his aggressive pose. My arms may not be as bulky as his, but I'm not afraid of the man.

After a few moments of silence, he gives in and allows me to do my job. We may not be on our way to best friend status, but he at least respects me enough to let me do what I'm paid to do. I'm staring at the screen of my tablet when I hear someone else's voice.

"Hey, Call."

I'm typing away to update his chart when I hear the ogre huff.

"Are we done?"

I wave him off and wish him luck at the next event. Once I set the tablet aside and wipe down the table. I glance up to see the raven-haired man Lexi and the blond left with last night.

He's even more gorgeous up close and has at least three inches on me. The dark hair I imagined running my fingers through when I got home is covered by a black beanie. His charcoal gray eyes sear into my soul with the way he is staring. My brain short-circuits, leaving a pregnant pause between us while he blatantly rakes his gaze up and down my body. My dick twitches to life as he saunters over and makes himself comfortable on my bed. I mean my exam table.

"You look familiar." His voice is deep and gravelly as he continues to stare. "I'm Hoyt Beck."

The man introduces himself as if his name isn't known around here. The KOC undefeated heavyweight champ. I swallow hard when he removes his shirt. How the hell did I not recognize him last night?

"It's my first day, and I just moved here." I shrug, not giving in to his attempts at flirtation. Instead, I remain professional, at least I tell myself I am. After I introduce myself to him, Hoyt allows me to go through the motions and complete his physical. My heart nearly thuds out of my chest as I type up the information needed in his chart.

His eyes haven't left me since he stepped into the room. My throat tightens at the way he seems to be evaluating me as well. Just not for the same reason I had him.

"You're good to go. Good luck at the match." I say to Hoyt, just like I had to Callum. Only this time, my voice is much huskier and filled with an obvious lust that wasn't there earlier.

A breath whooshes out of my lungs as the beautiful man exits my space. Jesus, what the hell was that? My inner monologue bashes the intense reaction my body has around Hoyt when I hear a throat clear.

"Hey, Doc."

I spin on my heel when I hear Hoyt's deep voice again. I cock a brow, silently asking what he wants when the man winks at me, just like he did last night.

HOYT

I've been unable to wipe the smirk off my face since I realized why I recognized the sexy as hell doctor. Hell, except for Gavin, all the docs come on to me at least once during each physical. Not Doc Dawson, though. He was reserved and barely looked me in the eye. It was jarring.

Most people act over the top to get my attention. Until I take them to bed. Then they turn meek and mousy, only wanting me to throw them around and give them pleasure. Don't get me wrong, I love the life I have. Every new town is a new experience and a new hookup. The knowledge that every partner I've had since I reached this level has only seen me as a challenge to conquer is getting a bit old.

The thoughts of Doc Dawson has me bouncing on my toes when I enter the penthouse. Corbin sits on the opposite end of the couch from Lexi. His focus is on fight footage of my opponent tonight. George is getting older and doesn't catch everything anymore, so I'm thankful Corbin has my back too. The extra set of eyes helps me up my game for every match.

Lexi glances up from her phone with curiosity in her eyes but doesn't speak. My gaze stays on her as I lower myself next to her. She cocks a brow, waiting for me to speak. When I don't give her what she wants, she folds.

"What?" Her question is full of accusation, which only makes my smirk turn into a full grin. Lexi's arms cross over her chest protectively as she waits for me to speak.

"Tell me about the guy you were dancing with last night." I waggle my eyebrows at her.

A flush covers her cheeks, making her an easy read as she recalls the events of the previous night. She never hangs around when people swarm us. I know sometimes women can be catty, but if I notice it, I cut that shit off at the head. She knows I'm not looking to settle down with anyone looking for a hookup, so she avoids them and does her own thing. Last night, that thing was dancing with any single man she could get close to.

"Uh, which one?"

She knows damn well which one I had my eyes on because she caught me multiple times from my seat in the VIP lounge. It was the only one I couldn't stop staring at when she was on the dance floor. I roll my eyes and slap her bare thigh, not realizing she had on booty shorts. Although I should have, given how much she likes to taunt Corbin. Lexi's hand lands on my chest with a returning whack.

"Ouch, asshole!" She groans and rubs her leg.

"Woman, you've nut tapped me harder than that when we're playing checkers." I glare at her before returning to the subject at hand. "The man Corbin had to drag you away from."

A fond smile curls her lips when she makes the connection.

"Oh, Xander. He was a blast." She recalls, "All I know is he's new in town. It was too loud to get much more information."

Dr. Xander Dawson. I file that information away for later. My lack of verbal response leads to another smack in the chest as her impatience grows.

"Guess who the new doc is." I pull my phone out of my pocket and lay it on the coffee table in front of us so it's not digging into my thigh.

Lexi's excitement is apparent at the potential of a new friend. Sometimes I forget she likes people as much as she does, considering how she avoids the crowds that form around me and Corbin.

"That's awesome! I'll swing by and invite him over for the after-party so he's not alone."

She stands from her spot next to me and walks into the kitchenette as I follow behind and sit on the bar stool.

"It has to suck being in a new place on your own."

"You're right," I say with my tone even.

Lexi turns to face me with a wide smile spread across her face until she sees that I'm still grinning.

"Oh no, never mind. I know that look. He's a nice guy, Hoyt."

A low groan sounds from her as she walks back toward me with a bottle of water in hand.

"Don't break this one."

"What the fuck is that supposed to mean?" I stare at her with my mouth agape.

An answering glare is the only response she gives me.

Xander

An intense and chaotic energy consumes the arena as Gavin leads me to the tunnel. There's a set of TVs mounted so anyone working the back can keep an eye on the fight without being ringside. It helps us gauge how bad a potential injury could be and gives us a different insight than those of the ringside doctors.

Our afternoon, once all the physical exams were done, was consumed with his expectations. He caught a glimpse of how I handled dealing with Westbrook today and said he has confidence I'll do well in whatever the athletes throw my way. If I'm honest, it was a relief to hear, given how little conflict I had to deal with in my last position.

Gavin tries to go on about protocol, but it's hard as hell to hear with the nonstop chanting while we gear up for the first fight. Nothing too intense happens during the first match, however, the second has someone on the mat with their arm bent in an unnatural position. Shit, I wanted excitement. Looks like I got it. There isn't much we can do here for that kind of injury. So after a quick stabilization, we transport them to the ambulance bay where the EMTs park.

For the first time in years, I'm thriving on the chaos that I find myself in. After we finished up with the most recent injury, my attention has been locked on the screens. Until I notice a group of people coming toward us out of the corner of my eye.

I sense him before my gaze finds him. Hoyt doesn't speak to me, instead, he shoots a flirty wink before vanishing into the madness of the arena. The same man from last night and an older gentleman follow Hoyt closely. Lexi, even though she's a tall woman, is still hidden behind their giant frames, only coming into view when she's next to me.

"Oh, my god! Hey!" she squeals and envelopes me in a hug. "I was hoping to run into you!" Her hands press against my chest as she pushes me to the side and out of the way of the walkway before she rushes off. "I'll come find you after the fight so we can exchange numbers!"

I have no time to respond. She chases after the three men who disappeared into the crowd when Hoyt's name is announced. Deafening roars sound as the match begins. My heart pounds erratically like a snare drum in my chest while the scene before me unfolds.

I bounce between watching the screen and watching the cage as I take in the fluidity of his movements. Hoyt is chaos and grace combined. The impact of his beauty and strength is awe-inspiring. Unable to tear my gaze away, I hope all my thoughts aren't written on my face.

"You're here to do a damn job. Not drool over the fighters," Gavin snarls and gestures to Hoyt's opponent. Driftin Marino is on the ground surrounded by the five ringside doctors.

My heart stutters in my chest at his comment. Unfortunately, or maybe fortunately, I have no time to overanalyze.

"Yes, sir." I nod and rush to meet the two docs who are helping Driftin into an exam room.

We spend a good bit of time tag-teaming the potential injury to ensure nothing will have lasting damage. Unfortunately for him, he has a concussion, which really is nothing new in this line of work, but he'll be out of commission for a minimum of one month. The dude got knocked upside the head so hard he wasn't even fighting the time off. His two ringside docs guide Driftin to stand, and before they leave, a blur comes bounding into the exam room.

Lexi hops onto the table like she owns it and nearly slides off like a cat who just inhaled an entire bag of catnip. Driftin chuckles and offers her an elbow, which she gently bumps with her fist in greeting.

"Nice moves, man," she praises, eliciting a flush along his cheeks as he moves out of the room and is led back to the locker room where his entourage waits. My lips turn up into a smirk, I chuckle and shake my head. The man practically swoons over her.

"What's so funny?" Lexi darts an annoyed glare at me.

I hold my hands up in surrender as I explain my amusement.

"Babe, you have so many people smitten with you and you don't even realize it. That guy from the club last night wouldn't take his eyes off you the entire time we were dancing." I chuckle again as I lower my hands and work to finish the necessary paperwork before I can leave for the night when she replies.

"Jealous?" I glance up to find her waggling her eyebrows at me.

If only it were that simple.

"You're gorgeous, but no," I admit.

Lexi hops off the table and, with a teasing tone, asks, "Ooo, got a girl back home?"

My mind flashes back to the last person I dated. I actually officiated her wedding a month ago. With a shake of my head, I expand to where my thoughts are.

"No, I'm just not interested in anything. Especially not here. I can't risk my job."

Lexi positions herself directly in front of me. Her eyes locked on mine as if she's staring into my deepest and darkest secrets and fears. A wide, knowing grin spreads across her beautiful face as her blue eyes shine with mischief. It should worry me, but surprisingly, it's comforting.

"Don't worry, your secret is safe with me." She winks and loops her arm around mine. "Hoyt is having an after-party at the penthouse. Come, hang out for a bit and celebrate the win."

HOYT

A n ACRAZE song is pumping through the built-in speakers of the penthouse as I sit comfortably on the couch. My arms spread wide to rest on the back and a bottle of Heineken in hand as I watch the space fill with women and men alike. Everyone is dancing and talking all around me, and usually I enjoy a good after party, but tonight, I really need a chill evening.

Corbin is chatting up a blonde I saw hanging around the last time we were here. She's been trying to get into my pants for years, but there is something about her I just don't trust. Don't get me wrong, she's cute as hell, big tits, perky ass, and legs that won't quit. It's his willingness to entertain her that has my annoyance at an all-time high. My frustration only grows when a familiar pair approaches me. They're dressed in the skimpiest outfits I've ever seen. How the hell did they even get an invite here? I inwardly groan as I offer a kind smile in greeting.

"Paige. Donovan. It's nice to see you." I bring the beer to my lips, taking a long pull from the bottle before resting my arm back along the couch. "Did you enjoy the fight?"

Thankful for the reprieve when the two of them rave over each of the champs of the evening. As they ramble on, I notice my blue-haired bestie enter with the one guest I will enthusiastically welcome to the party. Dressed in a pair of dark wash jeans and a heather gray Henley that fits so snug against his arms and broad chest, he looks bigger than he is. Fuck, it looks sexy on him. I observe Lexi doing her thing, as she introduces Xander to all my inner circle. Well, the people that we hang out with the most when we're in Vegas. Really, only Lex, Corbin and George are my inner circle.

She guides him toward the open bar and I track Xander, not taking my eyes off him. He holds himself with such confidence but also has a shyness about him when he's surrounded by people. It's mesmerizing and my cock stiffens. The man has a hold on me I'm not sure how to handle. That's not something that will get him very far in my life, yet there's something that makes me need to be near him.

By the time Paige and Donovan get to my match, I stand abruptly, excusing myself from the conversation with the dynamic duo to make my way toward my friend and her guest. As I stride across the room, her eyes find mine and she's got a wicked grin on her face like she's keeping a secret. We can unpack that later. Right now, my attention immediately diverts to Xander. When I reach the two of them, Lexi rises on her toes to press a kiss to my cheek.

"Lay off the bimbos and himbos tonight," she scolds.

She turns to Xander, wrapping her arm around me in a side hug. "The last time he took someone to bed after a match, we nearly had to reschedule a damn fight because he strained a muscle."

Before I can respond, she pulls away and wiggles her fingers in a wave while blowing a kiss in my direction. Unable to fight the chuckle, I roll my eyes at her retreating form. When my gaze returns to Xander, he's staring at me with a cocked brow. As if he's trying to assess how serious Lexi was being. His heated gaze makes me squirm in my own skin. I glance away and unconsciously use the heel of my hand to rub out the tightness in my pec. She may be a pain in the ass, but she's not wrong.

Xander

W hen Lexi said an after party, I didn't realize there would hardly be any breathing room. Jesus Christ. I glance around the room nervously. I've never been one for crowds. Being from a small conservative town, it's been ingrained to hide who I am. Obviously, that's impossible amongst a group of people.

Comfort washes over me as Hoyt approaches us. His face barely took any hits, so it's almost impossible to know he was in the cage tonight just by looking at him. The gray sweatpants he's wearing leave absolutely nothing to the imagination, and a loose, white t-shirt hides just how defined his body is. Lexi rushes off not long after telling the giant of a man to stay away from the groupies here. Granted, she used a little more colorful language.

My eyes rake up his large frame and land on his chest, which he's trying to massage. My brow arches in question as I assess him. He flushes at being caught, which causes my lips to twitch into a grin.

"Are you alright?" I ask as I take a step toward him instinctively and gesture to where he's digging his palm into his pec. It looks like he's in pain.

He nods. "Yea, I'm fine. They're always sore after a match." He shrugs as if it isn't a big deal. "So, Lex mentioned you just moved to town. What brought you to Vegas?"

Unable to tear my gaze from his chest, I explain my previous position and desire to move from the east coast.

"I was getting frustrated with not having much to do and if I'm honest." I drag my hand through my hair, it's the first time I'm admitting this out loud.

"You don't have to share anything you don't want to, Doc." Hoyt's words, for some reason, have me ready to bare my soul.

"Had I stayed there, I would have transitioned into a different career, which isn't anything I wanted to do," I confess.

Hoyt's features soften with my confession.

"This opportunity came at the perfect time. A birthday gift for myself, a fresh start before I turn thirty." I chuckle and look up to find his eyes locked on me. "I figured it would be a good way to get the excitement in my life I needed and meet new people." I shrug.

The air around us changes as Hoyt somehow stands taller when he replies. "When is your birthday?"

My cheeks flush, unable to hide my embarrassment. I never celebrated my birthday before. It was always just another day, so sharing it with him feels intimate.

"Yesterday." The confession comes out as a whisper.

His charcoal eyes sparkle with a wicked glint as a mischievous grin spreads across his beautiful face.

"Well, damn. Happy birthday, Doc," he says louder than necessary, which causes a loud chorus of cheers and well wishes. I can't help but chuckle at his ridiculousness. Hoyt winks at me before handing me another beer and leads me from the bar.

Our evening proceeds with an ease I've never felt before. We get lost in conversation and ignore the rest of the party. At some point, one of his guests comes up to say goodbye, and he doesn't even acknowledge them. The guest, obviously annoyed with being ignored, makes a point of walking close enough to shove me as discreetly as possible, which is the only reason the outside world comes back into view for a short period. I'm not as big as Hoyt, but I'm not a small man. I spend enough time in the gym that I can hold my own, so the impact didn't do much of anything but pull my attention away for a second.

I set my beer down on the counter when I see that Hoyt is massaging his chest again. My demeanor instinctively shifts to exude dominance and control so quickly that he stops the motion and stares at me with uncertainty.

"What's wrong?" Hoyt's confusion is apparent when his voice raises an octave.

HOYT

"When is the last time you've had a pectoral massage?" His demanding tone throws me. He's been so reserved until now.

I raise a brow as I stare back into his breathtaking green eyes.

"What? Why?" The confusion in my voice is clear.

He rolls his eyes at me as if he was expecting the response.

"There is no reason you should be favoring your chest that much." Xander gestures to me where my palm is still massaging, which makes me freeze.

"I'm fine." I force out the words even though it's been getting worse.

No one has ever looked through my bullshit so fast in my life. Xander drops his hands at his side and lets out a huff.

"No, you're not. May I?" He offers his hand, which I take willingly.

The change in his demeanor still has me reeling. My dick doesn't know what to do. As I follow behind him down the hallway toward the bedrooms, I tuck my dick in the waistband of my pants, so the tenting isn't quite as obvious.

"Which one is yours?"

His question pulls me from my thoughts, and I point toward the end of the hall with the largest room. He walks in and makes himself at home as he looks around the room. I stand at the door waiting like it's not the place I've called home for the last few days.

Why am I acting like a teenager who has never seen a dick up close?

Xander turns to face me, with something he grabbed from the dresser in his hand. His expression sends a jolt of desire straight to my dick.

"Close the door, take your shirt off and sit." He points to the bench at the foot of the bed.

After doing what I'm told, I swallow hard and wait patiently. Xander's back is toward me as I sit in silence, anticipation building with every moment.

The click of a lotion bottle grabs my attention. He turns toward me as his hand hovers in the air under the opening and a long stream of white cream piles in his strong palm. Xander quickly closes the distance, leaving mere inches between us. I grunt when a loud slap lands against my sore pec. He's stronger than he looks. His hands glide across my skin as he finds every pressure point in my chest. Wet sloshing sounds echo throughout the room as he works the tight muscles.

"Fuck," I rasp through gritted teeth when his expert fingers dig in right where the pain is worst. My eyes roll to the back of my head when he climbs behind me for better leverage.

"That's it, let it out." His raspy voice fills the room with praise.

My shock at how much that turns me on is sent to the back of my mind when his warm chest presses against my back. The monster between my legs stands at attention and is hard as steel straining under my waistband. I've never been shy about how large I am, until right now as the head of my cock pokes out of my pants and lays flush against my belly. There is no concealing how aroused his expert touch is making me. If Xander's eyes land on my groin, he's going to get an eye full.

Xander's strong fingers dig into my muscles, working out every bit of tension and pain. Unable to keep my noises to myself, grunts and moans of pleasure escape with every pass of his masterful handling of my body.

"You're doing so well for me," is the final straw. I lose my inner battle of control and my heavy balls tighten. I let out a low moan as my climax comes quickly and I explode, shooting up my stomach and chest.

"Fuck me," I curse, my cheeks flush. "I'm so sorry. That's never happened before."

Xander steps in front of me with a sinful smile. He presses my shoulders down so that I lay on the bed. Before my brain can catch up with what's going on, his tongue laps up the evidence of my release. I whimper—a sound I have never made in my entire god damn life—at the sensation and just how fucking hot his reaction to me unloading on myself is.

I attempt to drag Xander into the bed with me. My need to return the favor in some way has my skin on fire. He chuckles as he stands to his full height. The pride in his expression is intoxicating.

"The way you move in the ring may have kept my dick hard as stone all night, but this wasn't about quid pro quo."

He chuckles darkly as he presses his palm to my cheek, fingers tugging gently on my short beard as he stares into my eyes like he doesn't want to leave.

"Right now, you're staring at me like you have something to prove. And baby boy, you may be the big man out there but when you're with me. I'm in control."

Xander's hand falls from my cheek as he retreats to the door. I don't take my eyes off the curious man as he pulls the door open and winks at me before disappearing into the hall leaving me alone with my thoughts.

What the fuck just happened?

HOYT

M y morning has been a cluster fuck of confusion. I spent the first hour of the day jerking off in the shower like some teenager finding my dick for the first time.

How in the fuck did this happen?

While my excitement mounts in hopes of seeing Xander again, I'm not sure how soon it can happen, since the next fight isn't for a few weeks. I don't even have his number. Fuck, I've never been in this situation of having to work for someone's attention. Suddenly I feel like a dick for letting people fawn over me over the years.

A loud knock against the bedroom door snaps me out of my own thoughts.

"I'm alone. Why are you knocking?" I holler at the closed door. "Get your ass in here."

The latch clicks as the knob is turned and an adorable giggle echoes through the space. My lips turn up at the corners when Lexi plops onto the bed next to where I'm sitting to pull on my socks. When I turn to face her, she's got a silent plea in her eyes she knows will get her anything she wants.

"What is it?" I grumble.

She sits up and wraps her arms around my neck.

"I want to go for a hike, but Corbin and George are working on some new training ideas for you." She bats her eyelashes, which makes me snort.

I stand and drag her up with me, setting her back on her feet.

"Get your shoes, let's go." A chuckle rumbles from deep in my chest.

Surrounded by bright, blue skies with the afternoon sun beating down on us, I should be more present than I am. Lexi has been leading the way through the trails when usually it's the opposite way around. My scattered thoughts have me uncharacteristically quiet, so I shouldn't be surprised when she stops short with her arms crossed tight in front of her.

"What is your malfunction?" she snaps and taps her foot as she waits for me to respond.

I step around her and suck in a lungful of the fresh desert air, doing my best to ignore the line of questioning. Thankfully my legs are longer and just a few strides will give me a minute of peace. Even though I know she'll follow and the questions will continue. I move up the steep formation of rocks which lead to the top of a ridge.

The moment she reaches the top, she rushes around me to keep me in place.

"It's nothing." My eyes must betray me because she loops her arm around mine and drags me to a large rock that protrudes out of the side of the mountain, forcing me to sit with her.

I take in the beautiful surroundings for the first time today. A mixture of red and orange make up the desert scenery. It's not the first time we've been on this trail, but it's been a while since we've had the down time between events in one city that we could come out.

"Yea, ok." Lexi's snort is really more adorable than it should be. "What happened when you and Xan disappeared last night?"

The mask of stoicism must fail because she can see straight through me, just as she has our entire lives. Well, it doesn't help that my chest and cheeks heat under her inquisitive gaze. Her jaw drops, and she squeals so loudly it echoes through the desert.

"I didn't think he had it in him!"

Her giggles only seem to intensify the more she watches me. Lexi jumps from the rock we're sitting on and dances around excitedly.

"Wait, you knew he was gay and didn't tell me!" Unable to hide my shock as I confront my best friend.

Lexi's demeanor changes as she responds, "It wasn't my business to tell." Her soft tone cuts through my shock. "You, of all people, should understand that."

Her not-so-subtle reminder about how I was treated by my foster parents before George took me in.

I groan and lean back on my elbows as she looms over me. She quirks a brow as she assesses me from head to toe.

"Besides, I told you not to bang anyone." She throws her hands up, obviously frustrated with me. "Are you even up for this hike?"

My cheeks and chest burn even more. Damnit, how does this one man of all people have me reacting this way? I sit up and bury my face in my hands. Completely embarrassed by my reaction to her question.

"Oh, my god. What did you do? What the fuck happened?" She rapid fires in response. "You've never had a reaction like this when your sex life has come up. And dude, we've shared everything. Including a goddamn groupie."

A pregnant pause passes between us when I glance up at her from between my fingers. I can tell she's lost in the memory of that night.

"Ahh, he was a great fuck."

I grin as I remember that night as well.

"And his mouth skills were wicked good," I confirm.

The lack of amusement in my attempt to divert the attention away from Xander and I is apparent when she puts her hands on her hips like a mom about to scold their toddler.

"Yes, exactly! So why the fuck are you just now telling me you hooked up with him?"

I let out a frustrated groan. How the hell can I even explain what happened when nothing really did happen?

"Because we—" I begin, unable to figure out how to finish the thought. I try again. "I mean I didn't —" My voice cuts off before I attempt again. "He . . . We-I-ugh!"

Lexi's face is redder than a lobster straight out of the steam.

"Hoyt Evander Beck!"

I've never seen her so frustrated with me. My wall crumbles and I share everything with her. The way he touched me, the way he didn't touch me, and everything in between. To say she's in shock is an understatement, but by the time we're back to the car, she's got a wicked grin on her face that makes me nervous as fuck.

Xander

oyt's heated skin under my fingertips has haunted me since I left him last night. The way he became pliant under my touch and melted into me filled my body with a need I wasn't prepared for. I'm surprised he didn't feel my own erection pressed against his back as I massaged him. God, the sounds he made from just the touch of my fingers had me near the edge myself.

Last night may not have been the first time I've made someone climax from a massage, but it's the first time I had that intention going in. I couldn't resist after Lexi's comment. Everything about him had me ready to take him in a way he's clearly not used to and goddamn, it's hot knowing I have more experience than he does in at least one way.

My cock twitches as I lay in bed, reliving last night's events. Thankful that I crawled into bed naked, so there's nothing in the way when I slide my hand under the sheet and grip my aching dick. A low groan passes my lips as I stroke my length.

The memory of Hoyt succumbing to my touch and giving himself to me has my tip weeping with pre-cum. My hand tightens around the base as I continue pumping myself. Shallow pants fill the room when a sudden, harsh knock sounds from my front door.

I do my best to ignore the interruption as I recall the way Hoyt's eyes locked on mine when he came all over himself. The whimper when I licked up his release. My balls tighten as I continue fucking myself while the memories continue to roll. I feel the tingling at the base of my spine when the rapping at the door begins again.

"Son of a bitch," I grumble to myself as I stand up and drag on a pair of basketball shorts before tucking myself into the waistband and crossing the apartment to the door.

Gavin stands on the other side the corner of his eyes crease and a warm, genuine smile crosses his face.

"Hi?" I ask, in greeting, confused by his unexpected arrival. "I thought I didn't have to be in until Tuesday?"

Gavin's answering chuckle makes me a little less concerned.

"No, I was going to grab a bite to eat for lunch and I know you don't know anyone here, so I wanted to offer some company."

An excuse is on the tip of my tongue when an unmistakable grumble forces me to accept the invite; even if all I want to do is retreat into my fantasies.

Once I change into something that isn't likely to have my dick popping out, Gavin and I head out for lunch. Instead of driving, we walk a few blocks over to a tapas and sushi restaurant. The heat isn't quite as bad today, so the stroll over is enjoyable.

Gavin's thick, blond hair is a disheveled mess as we sit down for lunch. He drags his hands through the mane every few minutes while we speak. His tan skin is flawless, with virtually no sun damage in sight. You'd think he's closer to thirty just by looking at him.

The only tell of his age is the way he looks at me whenever a man walks by. His green eyes dart back and forth between us. While he gets that nervous energy about him that anyone over the age of forty-five back home would when they thought someone was gay. Gasp, not the dreaded g-a-y. I internally roll my eyes at the memories.

"Listen kid," Gavin begins. "I don't care who you date. I just don't want to see it." His eyes narrow on me while he continues. "If you hook up with the fighters, just don't be stupid about it and fuck around on KOC property."

My jaw falls at his words. Did he really just say that? I didn't think I was that obvious. No one in North Carolina ever confronted me about my sexuality. To say I'm shocked at his brazen remarks is an understatement. I shake my head as I try to make sense of the conversation. There is no way this man just went there.

Before I have a chance to respond, my phone vibrates in my pocket. When I pull it free, a chuckle escapes at the message.

Lexi

> I don't know what you did to this man, but he's begging me for your number.

Another text comes through before I have a chance to reply, which has my face heating.

Lexi:

I'm making him work for it. When he's done buying out this bookstore for me, would you mind if I pass along your info?

Being the smartass I am, I shoot back another idea for her.

Xander:

Make him rub your feet first.

Lexi:

Oo! I love the way you think!

Her immediate response brings me even more joy. I glance up to see Gavin staring at me with an accusatory gaze.

"Like I said, keep it off of KOC property." His features soften before he stands. "Let's get out of here. I've taken up enough of your afternoon."

He gestures for the waitress and hands over his credit card as soon as she approaches the table.

Gavin's attitude shifted as we walked back to my apartment. The way he talks about his family and kids is precious. He admitted his daughter came out as a lesbian recently and he's been learning more about the community and how to be an ally.

I chuckle when he apologizes about how he spoke to me.

"Kid, love is love and all that. I don't even like to see pictures of my wife and I kissing." He shudders at the thought. "I'm old school when it comes to PDA. What can I say?"

When I finally return home, I continue unpacking the rest of my belongings. The moment I finish putting away the last item in my kitchen, I receive a text. My brows furrow at the unknown number until I open the message. A wide smile splits my face.

Unknown:

So - are you a foot man or do you just like bossing me around?

HOYT

After buying one of every book at *xoxo Book Boutique*, a romance bookstore Lexi found, we *finally* came back to the hotel. I called down to the front desk to have boxes brought up so we can get the books shipped back home.

No sooner than my ass lands on the couch does she prance over to join me. Lexi bats her lashes at me as she lowers herself on the opposite side of the couch. She doesn't speak as she makes herself comfortable, her legs stretched out so that her feet lay on my lap. My brow arches in a silent question as I turn my head to face her. She's never been one for poker, so thankfully, she can't keep the amusement from her face.

"I can't do it, but the look on your face was priceless." Lexi's giggle fills the room. After she catches her breath and explains Xander's suggestion, she sends me his contact information.

My face breaks into a smile as I type away and hit send.

"I've never seen you like this."

Her comment startles me, but I shouldn't be surprised. I could feel her eyes boring into the side of my face the entire time I was typing. My lips part to respond, but I'm cut off when my phone vibrates in my hand. I stand up and retreat to my room as I read the message.

Xander:

> You know I like to boss you around, Baby Boy. The way you melted under my touch and praise tells me you enjoyed it, too.

My cheeks flush so badly at his text that I fan myself with my free hand as I reply.

Hoyt:
Want to come over so I can thank you for last night?

Xander:
I can't right now.

Hoyt:
What are you up to?

A picture of a wall mount and a tv that must be bigger than his arm span comes through, which gives me more of a reason to push.

Hoyt:
I can help.

Xander:
No, you won't. You're supposed to be resting today.

Hoyt:
Damn Doc. I've never enjoyed being told what to do until you had your hands on me. Let me take care of you when you are done.

Xander:
How about I let you come over and I'll show you just how bossy I can be?

Fuck me raw. I throw my head back while thoughts of what I'd let him do to me filter through my mind and groan as my cock instantly becomes stiff as stone. This man is going to be the death of me.

I feel Lexi's presence before I see her; I glance up just in time to see her standing next to where I sit on the edge of the bed. She's looking at my phone screen with a sinful smirk tugging on her lips.

"Bow chica wow wow." She waggles her eyebrows at me.

Lexi's laughter echoes through the suite as I jump up and rush out of the hotel room to get to a car.

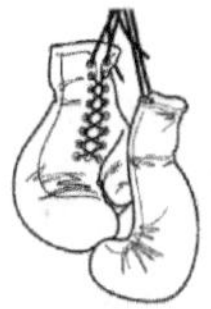

I tap the screen of my phone to pull up our text thread and confirm his apartment number. The sounds of classic rock greet me as I knock on the door. A smile spreads across my face when footsteps grow closer just before the door opens and I'm face to face with the man who has been at the forefront of my mind since he left me last night.

Xander's bare chest is on display and my mouth goes dry at the sight. Jesus, he's gorgeous. He's fit, not as bulky as me, but then I wouldn't expect him to be. But damn, he looks good. Unlike me, his skin is clear of any ink, at least that I can see. His mouth lifts in a wicked smirk as he steps aside.

"Come on in."

The deep tenor of his voice has a direct line of contact with my cock because it throbs in my pants with need.

I step inside the bright apartment and take in the beauty of the modern design. Hmm, my thoughts wander; I may need to do a remodel on my place back home. I feel Xander brush past me as he strides into the kitchen and grabs a couple of beers from the fridge. He tilts a bottle toward me, but I shake my head to decline the offered drink.

"No, thanks." I shake my head before explaining, "I drove over."

Xander's lips twitch at the corner as he fights back a smile. He carries both bottles with him as he crosses the room and sprawls out on the couch. His arms take up the back of the couch while he sits with his legs wide and waiting. When I attempt to follow, Xander cocks a brow, stopping me mid step.

"Wh-what?" I stutter with my gaze locked on the shirtless man staring at me from the other side of the room.

"Baby Boy, how often have you given control over to a partner?" Xander's eyes bore into my soul as he speaks.

"Never?" The answer comes out as a question. I'm not sure why.

"By choice or because they expect you to be dominant due to your size?"

His question shocks me. No one has ever been so direct with me. I swallow hard as a rush of heat coats my chest and face.

"That's what I thought."

Xander stares at me for a moment before he speaks again.

"Take your shirt off."

I still, contemplating my next move. Curiosity has me moving before my brain can catch up to my body. I drag the shirt off over my head and ball it up. Tossing it down next to me.

"On your knees."

Xander's eyes are dark with lust and desire.

"Crawl to me."

Xander

oyt's eyes go wide with shock. A mixture of excitement, confusion and desire war for dominance while he processes my instruction. Each emotion that graces his gorgeous face makes my cock grow harder, tenting my shorts.

My lips twitch when Hoyt balls his shirt up and tosses it on the ground. Charcoal eyes sear into mine as he slowly lowers himself to the ground and crawls on all fours across the room. My dick throbs with need as I take in the sight before me.

Hoyt pauses when he reaches me, laying his hands on his legs as he sits on his knees. Fuck. Me. He's beautiful. I lean forward and cup his cheek in my palm as he stares up at me.

"Tell me what you want." I urge him to voice his desires knowing that with his previous partners he's likely never been asked to do this.

My lips curl up at the corner when I see Hoyt's tongue dart out to lick his lips before he speaks.

"You," it's barely a whisper.

God damn, this big muscular man submitting only to me has my hand gripping my cock through my shorts trying to find some relief.

"I know that Baby Boy. But tell me, what exactly do you want from me?" My own voice is husky as I push him out of his comfort zone.

"I want to taste you." Hoyt's request comes out in a whimper and I'm nearly ready to blow from his words alone.

I spread my arms again across the back of the couch and nod at him, giving him permission to taste what he so eagerly wants. His hands brush up the outside of my thighs before he slips his fingers under the waistband of my shorts and pulls the fabric down just enough to free my cock.

Hoyt's breath skates over my skin as he dips his head to get closer to my dick. I fight back a groan of pleasure as his tongue swipes the head of my cock licking up the pre-cum leaking from my tip. His eyes stay locked on me as he lowers himself even more. Hoyt parts his lips and trails his tongue from my balls up the underside of my shaft to the tip of my dick, coating me in his saliva. I throw my head back against the cushions, silently praying to a God I don't believe in, that I hang on until I'm buried in his throat.

My eyes roll back when Hoyt's warm, wet mouth wraps around my cock and slides me deep into the back of this throat. I let out a low groan of approval while my hand darts out and laces through his dark strands. His facial hair tickles my sack every time his chin grazes my skin.

"Fuck, Baby Boy." I moan in appreciation.

His head bobs up and down my length in a practiced rhythm. His calloused hands palm my abs, feeling every inch of skin he has access to. Something about the feel of his roughness against my smooth skin sends me over the edge.

Unable to hold back any longer, my hands grip his hair, holding him in place while my hips buck. My cock grazes the back of his throat once, twice before unloading in his mouth.

My chest heaves with shallow breaths as I re-learn how to breathe.

Hoyt sits back on his heels with a shy smile directed at me. I lean forward and press my lips to his, savoring the way I taste on his lips. His hands latch on to my hair as he tries to raise himself and take over the kiss. I chuckle into his mouth and press my hands against his chest to push him off so I can stand, tucking myself away.

"Not yet," my expression hardens as I admonish him."Yo u'll get more when I tell you, you can."

His cheeks flush a beautiful pink and I wink at him, teasing him with the same taunt he'd been giving me as my hands drop to his jeans. My fingers work the button and zipper quickly allowing me to slide them down his hips. Hoyt sucks in a sharp breath when his cock is free from the pressure of his jeans. It takes every ounce of willpower I have not to lead him to my bed by his cock and fuck him raw. I glance up into his beautiful eyes and smirk before I step behind him and shove his jeans down to his ankles.

"Doc." Hoyt calls my name on a raspy breath.

Before he has a chance to argue, I guide him down so that his knees rest against the couch as wide as he can while the jeans are still around his ankles. His perfectly smooth and sculpted peach is in the air, ready for me.

His body stiffens when I settle between his legs. My hand falls, slapping his tight ass. It's cute he thinks he has a chance to hide from me. I kneel behind him and spit directly onto his tight pucker with no warning.

"Fuck, Doc!" Hoyt's words come out in a whimper as I swirl my tongue around his hole.

Working my tongue in and out, my hands massage his hips and ass driving him closer to the edge. His words come out in gibberish the more I lap at him. I swirl my tongue around a few times before I pull away to see his legs trembling underneath him and can't help but chuckle; knowing I'm the one driving him wild tonight.

"Doc, please."

The way he begs sounds so sweet and foreign coming from a man who is so used to being in control. Instead of giving in to what he wants I fuck his tight hole with my tongue for several more beats.

"Xander! God, please, let me ride you."

I still at his words, I thought I'd have to talk him into letting me take him. With one more flick of my tongue I stand. Hoyt turns to face me, his mouth crashes to mine as he grips his dick. My hand snakes up between us and I wrap my hand around his throat. He shudders as I pull away.

"Baby Boy, I'm still in charge. You're not going to come, until I tell you to."

I lean in and press my lips to his once more.

"Now, be a good boy and get rid of your pants while I grab a condom."

My feet move before he can stop me. Thankfully, I stashed a few boxes around the house when I was unpacking. I grab a foil packet and bottle of lube from the drawer.

Hoyt's pants are gone when I turn around. I can't help but chuckle. I stride back over to the gorgeous, tattooed man before me. His hands are on me in an instant as he hauls me to his chest and kisses the shit out of me. The moment I'm flush to him, Hoyt's dick is pressing into mine which is still covered by my shorts. He lets out a feral growl before he rips the fabric from my body.

"Well, God damn." I chuckle as I lower myself back down to sit on the couch.

Once I tear the foil wrapper open with my teeth and fully sheath myself, my eyes find his. The grey eyes I've become so fond of are darker than usual as I pop the lid to the lube open and pour a generous amount in my hand, covering my hard length.

Hoyt turns his back to me and lowers himself down, his feet are on either side of my hips as I guide myself inside him.

"Fuuuuck!" Hoyt groans.

I stiffen, unsure if he's taken too much. I know I'm not small, Hoyt places his hands on my knees as he pushes himself back up and lowers down again, taking in more of me.

"I forgot just how good this feels."

His groans turn into labored breaths as he continues to ride my dick. His tight hole clenching around me as his pleasure increases.

I place my hands on his sides, helping guide his tempo while he fucks himself using my cock. Jesus he's perfect. I feel a familiar tingling sensation at the base of my spine.

"Xander, I need to come."

Hoyt's plea has my cock begging for my own release, but I push him off my dick and spin the beautiful man around to face me. Shock colors his expression at the abrupt change, but before he has a chance to voice his frustration, my mouth is around his dick.

The need to taste the warm, salty goodness again is too great, and I pull him deeper into my throat. His hands dig into my hair as he thrusts into my throat once before his dick swells and he explodes into my mouth. The flavor of him on my taste buds sends me over the edge, and I moan with his dick still buried in my mouth as I blow my load into the condom still on my cock.

HOYT

X ander cautiously removes the second condom of the night and ties off the end before tossing it in the trash. His hand wraps around mine, leading me to a shower. He holds me close, pressing feather-light kisses against my chest while we wait for the water to heat. Once we step in, the sight of him slick with water has my dick standing at attention again.

If only my dick got the memo that my body is spent after the multiple mind-blowing orgasms from one man. Usually, I get bored and move on, which is why my sex life is generally filled with threesomes. Not with Xander though. I'm pretty sure I could go all fucking night.

"As much as I want you to paint the walls with your cum while I fuck your perfect ass," Xander whispers against my ear, his voice hoarse after the incredible head he gave me. "You need your rest, and I can see the exhaustion written across your face."

My shoulders sag in relief with his words. I'm so used to performing for everyone, even if it means I drain myself. I grip Xander's throat and tilt his face, so my mouth can easily access his. Our kiss is a frenzy of lust, tongues tangling in a heated exchange. I'm forced away when I try to grind my length against his stomach.

"You're not in control here, Baby Boy." Xanders grips my cock, and with a firm hold he stares into my eyes. "I'm going to tell you this one last time, I'm in control with you. You will get all the pleasure you can handle, but right now your body needs to rest."

His words are met with a needy whimper. From me. The current KOC heavyweight champion. What the fuck is he doing to me?

Xander drags me out of the shower and dries me off the best he can before he points to his bed. My heart stutters in my chest; I've never stayed the night with anyone. Why is it that I suddenly want not only to feel him close to me, but I need to be close to him? My feet carry me toward the large king-size bed, I glance up to see restraint hooks on the headboard, and my dick flexes with a mind of its own. *Down boy.*

Once I'm settled in bed, I wait for Xander to join me. My eyes bounce around the room landing on pieces of furniture, artwork, and finally on the man stalking toward the bed. I'm unable to fight the urge to smile when he climbs in next to me and pulls my giant frame into his front as if I weigh nothing. His bare skin is warm against my back, his arm weighs me down, and he holds me tight against him. This man has turned me into the little spoon.

What. The. Fuck.

"I can hear your mind running rampant. Take a deep breath, and we can talk in the morning." Xander's deep chuckle reverberates through me and sends a shiver down my spine while somehow also soothing my anxiety. It doesn't take long before the steady fall and rise of his chest against me lulls me into a peaceful sleep.

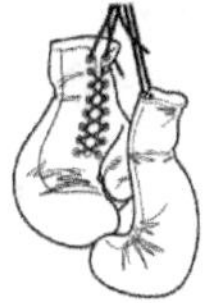

My eyes flutter open as a cool waft of air skates over my chest. Unfamiliar surroundings greet me until I remember I stayed over at Xander's. I reach behind me for him but find the space empty and cold. He's awake and must have been for a while.

I toss my legs over the side of the bed and begin my morning routine of stretching before I can attempt to act remotely human. I find my clothes folded neatly on a chair to the side of Xander's bed and quietly get dressed before I stride out of the bedroom. I find Xander in the kitchen slaving over a hot stove. My lips turn upward when I notice a plate with a fresh omelet, and the scent of oatmeal reaches me.

"Do you treat all of your hookups like this or am I special?" I ask teasingly, trying to hide my hopefulness.

Xander sets the plate with some mixed berries and a bowl presumably filled with oatmeal on the bar top in front of him. His eyes raise to meet mine shining with curiosity.

"Since you're only the second man I've been with..." He stops, allowing a pregnant pause for me to digest his words.

My eyes widen as what he admitted sinks in.

"I'm sorry, what?" I choke out.

Xander's cheeks flush under the scrutiny of my gaze while I wait for a response.

"I thought Lexi would have told you." His admission is quiet and shy. "I'm not... out."

I feel my skin prickle at his confession. There is no way I can deal with that.

"Listen, I can't hold your hand during that experience, Doc," I snap out a bit harsher than I meant to. The moment the words pass my lips I regret them.

To his credit, Xander doesn't flinch. His lips twitch like he's amused.

"I'm not asking you to." His gravelly voice bathes me in comfort as he rounds the counter. "I'm perfectly fine having this be exactly what it is. A good fuck every once in a while."

I open my mouth to say something, but Xander steps in front of me and presses his mouth against mine to silence me. He grips my dick through my shorts as his mouth urges me to open for him. Everything about this exchange is so much sexier than it should be. Xander kisses the ever-loving shit out of me, and I forget how to breathe for a moment when he finally pulls away.

"I know I'm not special. It doesn't mean I can't enjoy my-self until you decide to move on."

He presses another kiss to my lips, this time just a quick peck.

"Now, be a good boy and eat your breakfast." Xander's deep chuckle while his hand is still wrapped around my cock has me stiffening, ready to be whatever he needs me to be in this moment.

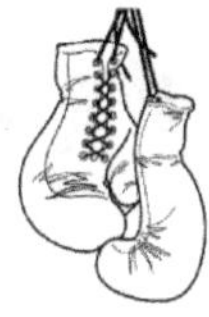

A week later

Corbin and I have been dancing around each other for the past hour. My energy level has gone to shit since we left Vegas after the last fight. Xander and I spent a few more nights together, but he vanished after the night of the last fight. We haven't spoken since, and it's been affecting me more than I care to admit. A fast fist hits my jaw and knocks me on my ass. *Fuck.* I shake my head to clear my mind before I stand.

"What the hell, Hoyt?" I hear Lexi gripe under her breath.

Corbin swings again, hitting me in the stomach. I hunch over and groan as I cough and try to catch my breath.

"Has your dick not been getting enough attention that it's affecting your game because I've never seen you so off balance," he taunts.

"Fuck off." My response comes out as a snarl as I sloppily unload on him. Corbin gets out from under my fists too easily as Lexi steps up to the ring.

"What in the actual fuck, man?" Her sassy attitude drags my attention from my friend who backs away from me.

I cock a brow at Lex and wave her off.

"Fuck that, what is the malfunction because, bro, I've never seen you like this." Her tone becomes frantic. "You're going to get hurt out there!"

I let out a low groan and stride to where Lexi is standing and take a seat next to her.

"I've never felt so at home with someone." The words come out on a groan. "You know me, Lex. There's never been anyone I stayed the night with before."

She wraps an arm around my shoulder as I continue.

"Shit, I've never even been with just one person at a time." I drop my face into my hands.

Lexi giggles while I explain my situation. I drag my hands down my face and scratch through my beard while my eyes lock onto hers. She holds her hands up as she stifles more laughter.

"I'm going to be honest with you. Apart from gramps, who is your longest relationship?"

When her blue eyes sparkle with mischief before she allows me to answer, I realize this is her monologue moment.

"Spoiler; it's me. You don't realize just how much you push people away." A smug smile takes over her face. "Hell, the only reason I've been your best friend as long as I have is because I burrowed my way into your life to the point you had no choice but to love me, and you're unable to live without me."

My eyes are locked on Lexi as I think back over the years she's been in my life. It's true; I tried to avoid her when we were younger. Any time I spent with her grandfather, my goal was to steer clear of her, but she never let me. She has always been around.

"Yea, I'm a ninja." She waggles her brows while imitating *Johnny Lawrence*. "You need to admit your feelings to yourself before you lose him."

Xander

R adio silence.

That's what I've heard the past week from my fighter. I scoff to myself. He's not mine, and he made that clear. I even told him I was ok with it. Why the hell am I so twisted up about this?

When he left for his next fight, I didn't expect some grand romance. It was some of the best sex of my life. Maybe I was hoping for some communication; friendship would have been nice. Not him pulling a Patrick Swayze and leaving his best friend to befriend me.

Lexi has been in constant contact, but she's made a point not to bring him up and vice versa. I'm thankful for that friendship because she's one of the few people I don't have to hide my truth from. Except maybe the fact that I would like more than just a good fuck with her best friend.

Speak of the devil.

The mix of emotions I feel over this are strange. Excitement and trepidation flow through my veins while her words sink in. Hoyt will be here in a week.

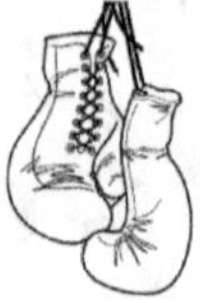

My heart thrums quickly in my chest as I step out of my car in anticipation of tonight. Gavin and Parker have already finished with the physicals for tonight's event, while I enjoyed a morning off. I stride through the doorway of my office and drop my bags on the chair. Once I press the power button to boot up my computer, I meander over to the coffee bar and make myself a cold brew.

Should I be drinking coffee with how anxious I am? Absolutely not. However, if I want to survive tonight, it's a necessity. Once I return to my desk, I take a seat and mindlessly scroll on my phone for a few minutes until there's a knock on my door. My eyes raise to find Gavin waiting with a cautious expression on his face.

"Why do you look like someone slapped your pet chinchilla?"

My brows raise at his question, and I sit back, straightening in my seat.

"I don't have a pet chinchilla?" The statement comes out as more of a question.

Gavin's deep chuckle brings a smile to my face.

"I mean, you look like something is wrong." He waves his hand at me like I'm wasting his time. "Let's go, you're cage side tonight."

The blood drains from my face. Fuck me. Of course he'd put me in the middle of it tonight. I stand and silently groan, then follow him out.

An overwhelming roar of excitement from the crowd makes my anxiety grow. While I do my best to ignore the internal turmoil of my emotions, the first contenders approach the cage. It's not the first time I've been this close since starting a couple of weeks ago. And every single time, I can't help but recall the way that Hoyt's movements had me in a trance from the jump.

Each round goes by quickly, blood is spilled, and the crowd cheers. Though I know his fight is up next, I've pushed it out of my mind. Until I feel his eyes on me, that is. I have no chance to respond before Lexi rushes up behind me and wraps me in a hug.

"Xan!" she squeals when she reaches me. "I've missed you. We're still doing dinner tomorrow, right?"

My lips turn up into a wide smile when she pulls away.

"I've missed you too, Babe." I'm unable to stifle a chuckle. "Yes, I've been looking forward to it all—week." I stumble over my words when I see him.

"See you later!" Lexi chirps.

Hoyt looks as beautiful as the last time I saw him. I nod in greeting and let out a heavy sigh before turning back to face the cage.

"Hey, Doc." I hear his smooth voice just as I feel his bare chest brush up against my back. My body goes rigid.

"Hey, it's good to see you. Good luck tonight." My response is short and to the point as I excuse myself and walk over to the other medics.

The next few minutes are spent with Gavin and Parker discussing how badly Hoyt is going to destroy his opponent, Booth. If I were a gambling man, I'd put my money on at least a broken eye socket. We're silenced when the first round starts, and Hoyt is barely able to avoid being taken out within the first few seconds. I glance toward Lexi who is on the other side of the cage with a grimace on her face. What the fuck?

The fluidity of his movements that had me drawn in a few weeks ago are gone, replaced with chaotic and slow reactions. At the end of the round, I rush up to where Hoyt is seated and kneel before him to check his injuries.

"What is going on out there?" I whisper as I clean him up.

Hoyt's pained laugh startles me.

"Why are you acting like you care?" he spits out at me. "You bailed on me before I left last time."

I recoil and look at him for a half a second, realizing we're in public, and go back to the task at hand.

"What are you talking about? I was trying not to crowd your space." I lean back and stare at him for what feels like a lifetime but must only be for a second, then realize that he's not used to being the one to reach out first, and the silence suddenly makes sense. I lean in and whisper into his ear, "I thought our fun was over when you left. If you want this, go out there and fight for me. Kick that guy's ass, and we'll talk after, Baby Boy."

The light returns to his eyes when I stand and go back to where I've been watching. I hold my breath when the next round starts. Part of me is expecting Booth to knock Hoyt out in a matter of seconds, but something clicks in Hoyt's demeanor. The fluidity that I saw in him before is back. The man gracefully lands the most powerful and smoothest power-roundhouse kick against the side of Booth's face, landing him on his ass.

Hoyt is pulled off his opponent, and his gaze immediately lands on me, a smile in his swollen eyes.

HOYT

Annoyance seems to be the theme of the evening. The first time I laid eyes on Xander he was wrapped around Lexi. It was the only time in my life I've envied someone touching one of my partners. On top of that, he acted like we didn't share something when I was here a few weeks ago. Like I was just another fighter or patient. Fuck, it pissed me off. I know damn well that's why I fucked up in the first round. The man got in my head.

Xander disappeared with Booth an hour ago. Logically, I know he has to make sure the dude is ok, but I hate that he's not with me. The moment I was able to rush off, I left everything with Lexi and dipped out before anyone had the chance to grab me for a damn after party. Now, I'm sitting outside his apartment waiting for him to get home.

My legs are sprawled out in front of me, taking up most of the hallway. Bright overhead lights make it impossible to relax even with my eyes closed and my head leaning against the wall. The sound of footsteps drawing closer makes my eyes pop open as I stare toward the entryway.

"You are a sight for sore eyes, Doc." A wide grin spreads across my face as I struggle to stand.

Xander shakes his head with an unimpressed expression while crossing the distance to help me. Once I'm on my feet, I take his face in my hands and crash my lips against his. He parts for me, obviously needing this just as bad as I do. A low growl emanates from his chest as he takes control and pushes me backward against his door. The sound of jingling metal pulls me out of the kiss, only to find Xander fumbling with his keys.

"Fuck, I've missed you, Doc." I pant when he pulls away to unlock the door.

The door swings open, and I fall backward. Xander is quick on his feet and spins around so that he takes the brunt of the fall when we land on the ground. He lets out a pained, "Oommf."

"Shit." I scramble to my feet, ignoring the soreness from tonight's fight. "Are you ok?" I ask as I help him stand.

The moment Xander is back on his feet, his eyes turn molten. He kicks the door shut behind us and wraps his firm hand around my throat, gripping me in a way that sends all my blood straight to my cock. I swallow hard against his hold. Fuck. I'm fucked.

"Baby Boy, you're going to need to remember that when you're with me... I'm in charge." Xander's voice is gruff as he scolds me. "If it were any other day, I would make you get on your knees as punishment. However, because of what your body has been through tonight, I'm going to let you in my bed." His hand drops back to his side as he nods toward the bedroom.

It takes every bit of my self-control not to strip on my way to the bedroom. A low groan rumbles from my chest as I fight the urge. But knowing how much this man likes to be in charge, I hold myself back. Once I enter his space, I take in the familiar surroundings. I may have only spent a few days with him before, but it feels like coming home. I turn to face the man who has my mind racing and my cock throbbing. Xander stalks toward me like a predator about to pounce. My dick jerks from its confinement of my shorts in approval of the sight before me.

Xander gently presses his lips against my throat while his hands dip under the waistband of my shorts, and he slides them down my hips. This gorgeous, dominant man drops to his knees before me as my cock springs free just in time to feel his warm breath against the sensitive skin. I glance down to find him staring up at me. The sight of him kneeling for me is almost too much. His hand darts up to stop me when I reach for my cock, needing to feel some relief. A sinful smirk crosses his lips as he leans forward and gently kisses the tip of my dick. My chest rumbles with a guttural growl in response. I need more, and he knows it.

My eyes go wide when he stands and drags my shirt over my head, leaving me bare. Xander swirls his finger in the air, motioning for me to turn around, and I comply. He rests his hands on my hips as he urges me forward to the bed. Firm lips press between my shoulder blades as he guides me down onto the mattress. My annoyance at how slowly he's moving has me tense, which seems to amuse him.

"Baby Boy, we have all night." Xander's chuckle reverberates through my body as I relax into the mattress.

Time seems to stand still, yet also go by in a flash. His expert hands roam over every inch of flesh and muscle, working through every part of my body. The sexy doctor knows exactly what he's doing to me because every time he nearly sends me over the edge with his masseur skills, he stops and moves onto another part of my body. I never thought a massage could be so erotic until I met this man.

When Xander finally allows me to roll over onto my back to face him, my cock is leaking with pre-cum. A wicked grin spreads across his beautiful face as he continues his torturous methods, from my sore pecs, to my abs, down to my thighs and calves. Each time my cock jumps with appreciation for his handiwork, Xander licks his lips and, fuck, it is a delicious sight.

"Doc." I groan and throw my head back onto the bed. "Please!"

Strong hands grip my thighs as he digs into my muscles, massaging in the most delicious way. Another plea is on the tip of my tongue when his wet mouth wraps around my cock. My eyes roll back at the sensation.

"Fuck!" I grind out through gritted teeth while he takes me deeper.

Xander's tongue is flat against the underside of my cock as he slowly fucks his own face without letting me take control. I nearly see stars when I hit the back of his throat. A better man, a smarter man, wouldn't complain, but I am neither of those. I prop myself up on my elbows and stare down my body into his breathtaking eyes while he takes my dick like a champ.

"I want to pleasure you, Doc." The breathy words are bare-ly audible as he makes his point.

He reaches for my ankles and props them on either side of his shoulders. I hear a click of something that I can't bother to worry about as Xander swallows around my cock. My pants of pleasure turn into a guttural moan the moment I feel his lube covered fingers prod at my tight ring of muscle.

I lift my hips, thrusting into his mouth, which elicits an appreciative groan from the incredible man latched onto my cock. His fingers slowly enter me, exploring my tight hole. Echoes of the noises I can't stop making bounce off the walls back toward us. Xander scissors his fingers to loosen me enough to take him.

"Doc, please." My plea is met with his fingers finding that delicious spot inside me. My hips thrust up to fill Xander's throat once more, then I unload the release that I've needed to for longer than I care to admit. He swallows around my cock and sucks every last drop before he releases me with a proud grin.

"Good boy, now roll over"—he chuckles darkly—"it's my turn."

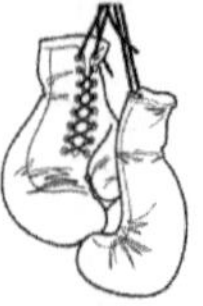

When I open my eyes to a feather-light kiss from my man, I'm surprised to also find a food tray straddling my legs. A raspy groan passes my lips as I scoot back on the bed to sit up. Xander's eyes are alight with emotion.

"Morning, Doc," I grumble and dip my head for another kiss. "You don't need to make me breakfast every time we're together, but if I'm honest, I've been craving your omelet for weeks."

He rolls his eyes at me before speaking.

"Get used to it, Baby Boy." Xander lies next to me, propped onto his elbow, watching me while I eat.

I cock a silent brow at him in question. I've never had someone take such pride in how they care for me. Unnerving? A bit, but I do enjoy it. We sit like that for a while with no words being spoken between us before I break the silence.

"Can I ask you something?"

I lift the tray and move it off the bed before I turn to face him.

"Yeah?"

My lips twitch as I stifle the grin that's trying to spread across my face.

"I've never been in a relationship. I know long distance is hard, but the past few weeks without you have been unbearable." My admission ends as I lean forward for another kiss. My lips brush lightly against his before I sit back up and continue my thought, Xander watching me with a hint of amusement in his eyes. "I don't know how to do this. But I do know I want to do this with you."

HOYT

Six months later

My alarm blaring pulls me out of a dream where I'm back in Xander's arms. I groan as I roll over and press the snooze button on my phone before throwing myself back onto the bed. The missed notification tone drags my attention back to the device. Once I disconnect the charger and type in my passcode, I see a message from several hours ago.

Those first few weeks, I traveled back to Vegas between every fight. It was glorious. Now, we're lucky to be on the same continent with how busy my schedule has been. Traveling to different countries and all the press tours mean we haven't been able to connect. Every morning is much the same as this one. I wake up to a text that Xander is going to bed just before I start my day.

My heart clenches in my chest, pained at just how much I wish we were able to talk and see each other more often. With a glance at the clock, I realize it's still late there, and I have a flight to catch. Selfishly, I ignore the time difference and press the call button.

It rings a handful of times before it goes to his voicemail, which he refuses to set up. After I disconnect the call, I pull up our message thread.

My flight was as uneventful as one could hope for, yet I'm still a mess the moment we are back on solid ground. I make my way down the stairs and breathe in a sigh of relief when I'm no longer confined in the metal tube of death.

Do I need to remind you of Final Destination?

I pull my phone from my pocket and see a missed call from Xander. Excitement floods my veins when I hit the call button to redial. After several rings, the call connects.

"Hey, Baby Boy."

My eyes sting with an emotion I'm still not used to.

"Doc, fuck, it's so good to hear your voice," I admit.

George, Lexi, and Corbin follow behind me as we head toward the transportation that's been reserved for our group.

"You'll be—" The line goes dead as soon as I step into the car and realize I've lost the signal.

"Fuck!" I groan through gritted teeth. "I'm so over this long-distance bullshit."

Corbin snorts out a laugh. "Dude, I'm shocked you've even lasted this long."

I glare at him over the seat and wait for him to continue, but it's George who speaks up this time.

"Kid, if you're gonna continue fighting, long-distance isn't going to work."

My phone notification goes off as we pull away.

Xander:

I tried calling back, but there must not be a signal there. I know you'll be back in a few weeks, but I miss you. We'll talk soon.

I throw my head back against the headrest and let out another annoyed huff. George reaches across the space and pats my knee. I glance at him to see a mischievous smirk playing on his lips.

"Since we have to spell it out for you… bring him on as your full-time medic, and he can travel with us." I hear Lexi giggle just before she slaps me upside my head.

"Ouch."

Xander

A week later

Sleep has evaded me the past few days, and my coffee isn't cutting it today. I'm too excited knowing that Hoyt will be here soon. Right now, Callum Westbrook is sitting on my exam table with an annoyed expression as per usual with this man. I yawn as I turn to face him and go through the same bullshit as every exam since we first met.

"Do you ever wonder why I fight you and not the others?" The question comes out with a grunt.

I roll my eyes and approach him with the vials and needles needed for the day's blood test.

"Because I'm the new guy." My tone is matter of fact.

Callum snorts and extends his arm for me to search for a vein.

"Because I saw the way he looked at you that first night at the club with Lexi. He's never looked at me that way." His confession has me stumbling backward a step. My gaze meets Callum's, whose lips curl up into a half smirk. "It was only a couple of times after we both won our matches, but he would never give me more than those couple of nights, and he always insisted we have someone else with us."

I stand, staring at my patient, who looks smug as hell at the admission. Hoyt's active sex life has never been something he's hid; I mean one look at the man, and you know there's a revolving bedroom door.

"Don't worry, Dr. Dawson. He hasn't touched anyone but you in over six months. I just wanted to get it off my chest since I'm fighting him tonight." Callum shrugs and holds out his arm in a silent truce.

What in the actual fuck.

Once I finish drawing his blood and place the vials on the metal tray next to me, I step back and stare at Callum. I'm not sure what exactly there is to say, but it feels wrong not to address what he said.

"I was a dick, and for that I apologize. Thanks for not letting my behavior affect how you treated me." The man stands up and winks. "Have a good one, Doc."

A throat clears, and I glance up to see a beautiful sight. Hoyt is standing before me in a pair of gym shorts with a bare chest.

"Do I need to kick his ass before the fight tonight?" His smooth-as-whiskey voice fills my ears and soothes my soul at the same time.

My lips turn up into a wide grin as I cross my arms against my chest.

"I'd rather you wait until it counts." I lift my shoulders in a shrug. Hoyt's long strides across the exam room have him in front of me in an instant.

"Speaking of..." His words skate across my lips. He grazes my cheeks with the pads of his fingers, and my eyes close as I lean into his touch. Before I have a moment to relish in the closeness, he tangles them in my hair and crashes his mouth to mine. His tongue sweeps along my lips, urging me to open for him. When I do, he takes the opportunity to swirl around my own. A needy whimper escapes my lips, and I wrap my arms around him and hold him close. I feel the length of his growing erection press hard against my stomach before he pulls away to take a breath. "Fuck, I've missed you, Doc."

My eyes flutter open, taking in the man before me.

"I've missed you too, Baby Boy." The confession isn't news, but it feels like I haven't expressed it nearly enough since it's been so long since we've seen each other.

Hoyt's eyes are bright with excitement before he turns his back on me and closes the door, then hops up on the exam table and hooks his finger, gesturing for me to come to him. I quirk a brow.

"Since when do you make the rules?" I chuckle but close the distance between us.

The smartass rolls his eyes at me but dips his head down and places a chaste, soft kiss against my lips.

"I have a proposition for you." He's smiling like the damn cat who ate the canary.

My eyes don't leave his as I wait for him to elaborate. My curiosity is killing me.

"Quit your job and come work for me? You can travel with us and still practice"—he waggles his brow at me suggestively before finishing his thought—"medicine."

I can't find the words to respond before Gavin calls for him to do his pre-fight physical.

The rest of the day is hectic, and we don't see each other again until it's time for the match to start. Lexi rushes up to me much like she did the last time we saw each other at the cage. Our interaction is brief because the moment I see him, I can't pull my attention away. Hoyt smirks at me as he strides toward me with purpose and leans in to speak directly in my ear, but I don't give him a chance.

"Get up there and kick his ass." I press my lips to the sensitive spot behind his ear, no longer caring who knows about us. "Fight for me, and I'll come with you."

Xander

M etal links clank on the ring attached to the headboard while I carefully strap Hoyt's left wrist in the leather cuff. A sinful smile pulls at my lips as I round the bed and secure his other wrist before he wakes. I make quick work of doing the same with his ankles.

His thick, muscular thighs are spread beautifully for me when I climb onto the mattress.

My cock has been half-hard since I decided to do this the night he asked me to go with him. The night he broke Callum's jaw in the final knockout.

I pick up the toy I'd laid next to his ankles and allow the soft leather strands to glide across his skin. Goosebumps trail behind the flogger, and a low chuckle rumbles deep in my chest when I gently slap the tail against Hoyt's thigh. He startles, and his gorgeous grey eyes open to stare up at me.

"Good morning," I grin, slapping his other thigh with the flogger.

Hoyt tries to pull his arms down from over his head only to be stopped by the restraints. A beautiful pink tint colors his cheeks when he glances up at his wrists, realizing that he's been cuffed.

"Doc…" he whispers the pet name he's called me since the day we officially met. It will be a rare treat for us to use my toys once we leave today. The bed is the last thing left to take apart, so I decided to wake my man up in a special way. We've talked about consent and what we're both open to; we've just never had the time to execute any of those desires.

"Be a good boy, and do as you're told." I wink at Hoyt before I bend down and press a soft kiss against his stomach. My hand grips firmly around his already stiffening cock. Thank God for morning wood.

A sweet whimper sounds above me when my tongue darts out to swirl around the head of his dick. I begin to stroke his generous length as I drag my gaze up his gorgeous frame to find his eyes closed. I wrap my lips around the thick monster between his legs and suck him deep into my throat, coating his length with my saliva. I stare at his face while he's touching my tonsils, slightly amused by the concentration etched across his face.

Reluctantly, I drag my mouth off his perfect dick, the savory flavor of his pre-cum on my tastebuds as I lift myself off. The most desperate moan leaves Hoyt, and his eyes fly open again. A smile dances across my lips as I swipe my thumb across his tip, spreading the juices that leaked out as I teased him with tongue.

"You want to come? Eyes on me, Baby Boy."

"Please!" Hoyt's whispered plea makes my now fully erect cock throb.

Leaning back down, I continue to run my tongue up the length of his dick, from root to tip, flicking the sensitive, silky skin under the crown. A sharp intake of breath fills me with pride when I see my man fighting the instinct to close his eyes.

My tongue darts out to moisten my lips before I slowly take him in again. Hollowing my cheeks, I suck him deep into my throat. Hoyt tries to thrust his hips to get deeper, but the restraints and my position on top of him keep him in place.

"Doc, please." His voice cracks through the pained request, and his fingers dig into the sheet-covered mattress, trying to find purchase as I continue to devour my favorite part of him.

My spit is pooling at the base of his cock, coating my beard with every bob of my head. Sliding my hand underneath him, I inconspicuously coat my thick finger in the saliva before gently massaging his tight ring of muscle.

"Fuck, Doc!" The sound of Hoyt's pleasure rumbles through his chest.

Pride fills me as his cock begins to swell and pulse in my mouth just before he finds his release. His gaze is locked on me when he comes, a perfect "o" on his lips as he pants through the intense pleasure.

I swallow every drop, wishing for more. There is just something satisfying about this man filling my mouth with his seed, and something about seeing my own dripping from his tight hole that I seem to need even more since we publicly claimed one another.

"Good boy." I wink at him while I kneel between his legs, a second finger inside him now, still massaging the sensitive spot that has his dick already ready for round two. "May I?"

"You don't need to ask. Fuck me, Doc."

I grip the base of my cock firmly with my free hand; the tip already coated with my own desire before carefully removing my fingers and slowly replacing them with my dick.

Hoyt's ankles may be restrained, but I can position his body well enough to slide inside him while he's on his back. That perfect "o" is back on his lips as he takes every inch of me.

"You are taking me so well, Baby Boy."

Hoyt preens under my praise.

He continues to breathe through the intrusion; my man may not be used to taking dick like this, but fuck does he do it well.

"Your ass looks so good taking my cock, Baby Boy." I grab the forgotten flogger from the mattress and slap his thigh, which makes him clench around me. My favorite fucking feeling. I let out a guttural groan of approval.

"Fuck. Me. Doc. Quit. The. Fucking. Torture." He makes sure to enunciate every word.

My lips pull at the corner, and I slam home. My cock buried inside my man's glorious ass is a sensation like no other. He's mine, all of him.

Slowly, I pull back before thrusting back inside him.

The room is filled with the sounds of our pleasure, every movement bringing us that much closer. Hoyt's eyes are still locked on me, doing exactly as he was told. My lips twitch into a sinister grin while I carefully slide my hand between us until my fingers land on his taint. His eyes go wide when I begin to massage the spot while still thrusting hard inside him. I can feel the sweet spot with every movement.

His cock visibly twitches and pulses, and his balls tighten more and more as I continue the delicious assault. Hoyt's pleas for another release are coming out in gibberish. I chuckle as he tries to fuck the air while I'm still inside him.

"You're such a good boy for me. Now I want you to cover yourself with cum, so I can lick it off you, Baby Boy."

I rasp as my own dick begins to pulse inside him.

"Doc!" he calls out my name again as we both empty ourselves.

The sensation of my cum shooting deep inside his ass has me ready to collapse. My dick twitches inside him when I realize just how much cum is on his chest. I gently pull out and lower myself to lick up every drop.

I reluctantly slide up the bed to remove all four cuffs before pulling him into my side. Hoyt's breathing is still not back to normal by the time he's released.

"Fuck, you are so good to me," he says through panted breaths, "I love you, Doc."

My heart swells at his admission. I might not be staying in Vegas as long as I planned, but I'm leaving with more than I ever expected to find.

Also by

Endgame

The Unexpected Series

The Unexpected Match Hadley & Connor's Story

The Unexpected FirstRyan and Greyson's Story

The Unexpected Reunion - Book one of Pickle's duet

The Unexpected ThirdBook two of Pickle's duet

The Unexpected Dance Pre-Order Alannah's story

Mafia

Ludovico's Vengeance

KOC Novella

Fight For Me – MM

Stand Alone - Dark Romance

KILLER IN OUR POCKET - MFF

Stand Alone – Small Town Romance

Pumpkin Spice and Mr. Right

Acknowledgements

My family, your support during this journey has been incredible.

To my Stupid Face Moron, ditto.

My alpha team, you are the MVP, and I can't imagine this journey without you.

Sara - My boo. I'll forever be thankful that you slid into my DM's. You are phenomenal, and I love you!

Brittany – From 0-2mil and for the rest of the ride. You are one of my favorite humans and I'm so thankful to know you…. & for Abelina.

Tana – I'll never be able to thank you enough for the way you've curbed the chaos that is my mind.

K.D. - My ride or die, I love you, and I'm so freaking proud of you!

My Street Team – Bestie Boo's:

Laura P., Jordon S., Brittany T., Jennifer L., Megan A., Brandy S., Nicole H., Ashley P., Lori L., Morgan H. Leigh U., Cheryl P., Jessi H., Tabs S., Haley E., Nicole W., Jasmine G., Jeanette R., Erin V., Becci T., Courtney C., Tiffiany S., Lindsey M., Nickol D., Veronica T., Sidhi B.

Without y'all I don't know where I'd be. You are the best group of people a girl could ask for. <3

To the FBI Agent who tracks my search history, it's been real.

Lastly, but most definitely not least, to every single one of you who has reached this page. There will never be enough words for me to express my love for you adequately. Thank you for reading my books. I can't wait to share additional stories with you!